STD

Chet the Pet

The dog ran toward the boys, wagging its tail.

"A golden retriever!" Joe cried happily. "Neato mosquito!"

But just as Frank was about to pat the dog, it shook its long yellow coat.

"This dog is sopping wet!" Frank cried.

"Yuck!" Joe sputtered. He shook his wet hands.

"Oh, no!" Mike gasped suddenly. "This is awful!"

"What's wrong, Mike?" Frank asked. "You look like you've seen a ghost."

"It's not a ghost I'm looking at," Mike said. "This dog is Chet!"

Frank and Joe Hardy: The Clues Brothers

Available from MINSTREL BOOKS

FRANK AND JOE HARDY: THE CLUES BROTHERS™

THE DOGGONE DETECTIVES

Franklin W. Dixon

Illustrated by
Marcy Ramsey

A MINSTREL® BOOK

Published by POCKET BOOKS
New York   London   Toronto   Sydney   Tokyo   Singapore

This book is a work of fiction. Names, characters, places and incidents are products of the author's imagination or are used fictitiously. Any resemblance to actual events or locales or persons living or dead is entirely coincidental.

A MINSTREL PAPERBACK *Original*

 A Minstrel Book published by
POCKET BOOKS, a division of Simon & Schuster Inc.
1230 Avenue of the Americas, New York, NY 10020

Copyright © 1998 by Simon & Schuster Inc.

Front cover illustration by Thompson Studio

Produced by Mega Books, Inc.

ISBN: 0-671-00409-3

First Minstrel Books printing September 1998

10 9 8 7 6 5 4 3 2 1

FRANK AND JOE HARDY: THE CLUES BROTHERS is a trademark of Simon & Schuster Inc.

THE HARDY BOYS, A MINSTREL BOOK and colophon are registered trademarks of Simon & Schuster Inc.

Printed in the U.S.A.

1

A Bark in the Park

Let's see you catch this one!" eight-year-old Joe Hardy shouted.

It was Saturday morning. Joe and Frank Hardy were playing Frisbee in the park with their friend Chet Morton.

"Try me!" Chet shouted back. "There isn't a Frisbee I can't catch."

"You asked for it," Joe said. He pretended to throw the Frisbee in one direction. Then he threw it in another.

Chet ran sideways. "I got it! I got it!" He leaped up and snatched the Frisbee.

"How does he do that?" nine-year-old Frank Hardy said.

"It's all in the wrist," Chet said. He flung the Frisbee back to Joe.

Joe was about to go for it when their friend Mike Mendez ran onto the field. The Frisbee landed on the ground with a thunk.

"Interference," Joe called.

"Hey, you guys," Mike said. "Check out my new invention."

Mike held up a gadget built from tin cans and telephone wires. The wires were connected to a tiny tape recorder that was strapped around Mike's waist.

Eight-year-old Mike was always inventing things. He had made everything from an automatic stamp licker to a shoelace untangler.

"Later, Mike," Chet called. "We're in the middle of a game."

"But this is a—" Mike said.

"Zack attack! Zack attack!" a voice called from the other side of the field.

Frank, Joe, Chet, and Mike turned to see a boy with spiky hair speeding toward them on a bicycle.

"Oh, great," Joe groaned. "It's Zack Jackson. On wheels."

Frank and Joe had moved to Bayport just before the school year had begun. By now they knew that Zack was bad news.

"Full speed ahead!" Zack roared.

The Hardys heard a loud crunch as Zack rode his bike over the Frisbee.

"That's my Frisbee, you dork!" Chet shouted as he ran over.

"A Frisbee?" Zack said. He jumped off his bike. "And all this time I thought a UFO had landed in Bayport. Ha-ha!"

Frank and Joe rolled their eyes. Zack was always messing with them.

"What goofy thing did you invent this time, Mendez?" Zack asked. He pointed to the gadget. "Something to make you cool?"

"Get a life, Zack," Frank said.

Zack folded his arms across his chest.

His arms were covered with stick-on tattoos.

"You wanna make a case out of it?" Zack asked Frank. *"Clues* Brothers?"

Zack knew that Frank and Joe Hardy loved to solve mysteries.

"Gotta fly," Zack said. He jumped back on his bike and started to pedal.

"Like a witch on a broom," Mike mumbled as Zack rode away.

Chet shook his head. "I hate that jerk more than I hate liver!" he said.

Mike held up his invention. "This will cheer you up, Chet."

"What is it?" Frank asked.

"You happen to be looking at the Mighty Mendez Beast-o-matic," Mike said.

"A what-o-matic?" Joe asked.

"It turns people into animals," Mike explained.

Joe's eyes popped open. "No way!"

"Listen," Mike said. He pushed a green button on the tape recorder. The boys heard a barking noise.

4

"Whatever animal I put on this tape is the animal you get," Mike said. "In this case, the person would turn into a dog."

"I like dogs," Joe said.

"Okay," Mike said. He pointed the Beast-o-matic at Joe.

"Whoa!" Joe said. He pushed the gadget away. "I said I like dogs. I don't want to *be* a dog."

All of a sudden the Beast-o-matic made a loud whirring sound.

"What's happening?" Joe asked.

"When you pushed it away, you accidentally switched it on," Mike said.

"And it was pointed at Chet," Frank said.

"Woof, woof," Chet said.

Frank turned to Mike. "Did you ever turn anyone into an animal before?"

"Nope," Mike said. "But there's always a first time."

Chet put his bent Frisbee under his arm. "I've got to get home," he said.

"Are you going somewhere today?" Frank asked Chet.

"Nope," Chet said sadly. "I just don't feel like hanging around anymore. I'm too upset about my Frisbee."

Frank, Joe, and Mike watched as Chet walked toward the park gate.

Joe whistled. "Wow. I've never seen Chet so down in the dumps."

The boys spent some time on the tire swings. Then they ran to the snack stand.

Frank dug into his pocket for change. He felt something bulky and squishy.

"Uh-oh," Frank said. He pulled out a plastic bag. "Chet asked me to hold his gummy worms. I forgot to give them back."

"Let's go over to Chet's house and return them," Mike said. "Maybe we can cheer him up, too."

Joe sighed. "It's going to take a lot of gummy worms to cheer Chet up today."

The boys left the park and walked the

few blocks to the Mortons' house. When they rang the doorbell, no one answered.

"Anybody home?" Joe called up to the windows. "Chet? Iola?"

Iola was Chet's seven-year-old sister. She didn't answer, either.

Frank looked at his watch. "It's twelve-thirty. Chet said he wasn't going anywhere today."

"And Chet always tells us everything," Joe said. They peeked into a few windows, but the whole downstairs was dark.

"Maybe Chet's Frisbee really *was* a UFO," Mike said slowly. "Maybe the Mortons were abducted by aliens."

Joe shook his head. "Earth to Mike! Earth to Mike!" he teased.

The boys checked all around the backyard. No one was there, either.

"Now what do we do?" Mike asked.

"I'll count to three," Frank said. "Then let's all yell 'Chet' really loud."

"Okay," Joe said.

"One . . . two . . . three!" Frank counted.

"CHET!" everyone called.

"WOOF! ARF! ARF!" was the only reply.

The boys looked around in surprise. A big dog dashed out from under the house. The dog ran toward the boys.

"A golden retriever!" Joe cried happily. "Neato mosquito!"

But just as Frank was about to pat the dog, it shook its long, yellow coat.

"This dog is sopping wet!" Frank cried.

"Yuck!" Joe sputtered. He shook his wet hands.

"Oh, no!" Mike gasped suddenly. "This is awful!"

"What's wrong, Mike?" Frank asked. "You look like you've seen a ghost."

"It's not a ghost I'm looking at," Mike said, pointing to the dog. "This dog is Chet!"

2

Mystery Mutt

What do you mean, this dog is Chet?"
Joe asked.

"Remember when the Beast-o-matic accidentally went off?" Mike said. "When it was pointed at Chet?"

"Sure," Frank said. "But we didn't see him turn into a dog."

"He could have slowly turned into a dog as he was walking home," Mike said. "Like in those werewolf movies. First comes the hairy face . . . then the claws . . . then the long, pointy teeth—"

"WOOF!"

The dog jumped up on Mike and began licking his face.

"Ahh!" Mike screamed.

"Mike," Frank said. "Just because this dog ran out when we called Chet, doesn't mean he *is* Chet."

Then Frank felt the dog nuzzle his back pocket. "What's he doing?" he asked.

"Frank," Joe said. "Aren't the gummy worms in your back pocket?"

"Yes," Frank said. "So what?"

"Aren't gummy worms Chet's favorite candy?" Joe asked.

"Proof number two!" Mike groaned.

Joe patted the dog's head. "If this dog *is* Chet, then why are the rest of the Mortons missing?"

"Maybe it's contagious," Mike said. "Maybe Chet turned them all into dogs!"

"No way!" Frank cried.

"I wonder where the Mortons really are," Joe said. He reached down to scratch the dog's wet ears. "And I wonder who this fella belongs to."

Frank ran his hand along the dog's neck. "He's not wearing a collar," he said.

"Then we can keep him," Joe said.

"Forget it, Joe," Frank said. "A great dog like this has to belong to someone."

"What do we do now?" Mike asked.

"First, we talk to people in the neighborhood," Frank said. "Then we ask Dad to find out if anyone called in a report about a missing golden retriever."

Frank and Joe's father, Fenton Hardy, was a detective in Bayport. He sometimes helped the boys with their cases.

"What if no one claims him?" Joe asked.

Frank shrugged. "Mom and Dad would tell us to solve the mystery."

"Another case for the Clues Brothers!" Joe cried. "Yes!"

The dog barked three times.

"Not so loud, Chet," Mike said.

"Will you stop calling him Chet?" Frank begged. "His name is . . . is . . ."

The dog chewed playfully at Frank's sneakers.

"Sneakers!" Frank said.

"Sneakers . . . I like it," Joe said.

"I've got to go home for lunch," Mike said. "Even though I feel sick."

"Cheer up, Mike," Frank said. "Meet us in the park at three. You can help us work on the case."

"Okay." Mike sighed as he rested his Beast-o-matic on his shoulder. "Bye, guys. Bye, Chet—I mean, Sneakers."

On their way home, the Hardys spoke to a few of Chet's neighbors.

"Is this your dog?" Joe called to a family in their yard.

"I wish it were mine," a boy called back.

The other people on Chet's block looked at Sneakers and shook their heads.

"Don't worry, Sneakers," Frank told the dog. "We'll find your owner soon."

"Not too soon, I hope," Joe said. "I've always wanted a dog."

Frank and Joe turned the corner onto

their street. "What if Mike's Beast-o-matic did work? You saw the way Sneakers went for those gummy worms."

"Give me a break. Not you, too?" Frank said.

"Just because we're brothers doesn't mean we have to think alike *all* the time," Joe said. "We don't even look alike!"

Joe was right. He had blond hair and blue eyes. Frank had dark hair and brown eyes.

The boys stopped at the mailbox in front of their house. Inside were bills for their parents and the latest issue of Joe's Gross Ghost Fan Club magazine.

The Gross Ghost was Joe's favorite action figure. When the magazine arrived, he usually read it right away. But not today.

"This will have to wait," Joe said, rolling up the magazine. "We've got a case to crack."

Frank pointed a finger at Sneakers. "Wait here in the yard, boy. We have to explain everything to Mom and Dad."

Sneakers tilted his head. Then he plopped down on the grass.

"Do I smell meatballs?" Joe asked as they walked into the front hallway.

Mrs. Hardy smiled. "There's a two-foot meatball hero in the kitchen."

Mr. Hardy came out of the den. "We thought you boys would like a treat."

"Um, Mom . . . Dad," Frank said slowly. "We have a treat for you, too."

"But our treat has four feet," Joe said. He tossed his Gross Ghost magazine on the hall table.

"Come with us," Frank said. He opened the front door again.

"What could it be?" Mrs. Hardy asked as they walked outside to the yard.

"Introducing Sneakers!" Joe announced. The dog ran over.

"Sneakers?" Mr. Hardy asked.

"Where did he come from?" Mrs. Hardy asked. She gently stroked Sneakers's ears.

"We found him under Chet's house," Frank said.

"He's very clean. He smells as if he's just had a bath," Mrs. Hardy said. "But since we don't know anything about him, he'll have to stay outside."

"Can we keep him?" Joe pleaded.

Mr. Hardy patted Sneakers's head. "Not if he belongs to someone else," he said.

"Dad, can you see if anyone's called in a missing-dog report?"

"Good idea," Mr. Hardy said. "I'll call the police station right now."

"Sneakers must be thirsty," Mrs. Hardy said. "I'll go inside for a bowl of water."

Frank and Joe left Sneakers outside as they followed their parents into the house.

"Suppose we never ever find Sneakers's owners?" Joe whispered to Frank in the hall. "Then Sneakers might really be Chet!"

"That would be terrible. Chet is our best friend," Frank whispered back.

Joe smiled. "Then I'll have a best friend—*and* a dog."

Frank laughed. "Chet is probably somewhere right now chowing down on one of his favorite foods."

Suddenly they heard their mother scream. Frank and Joe ran into the kitchen. The meatball hero lay on the floor.

"Oh, no!" Frank groaned.

"Sneakers ate all the meatballs out of the sandwich!" Joe cried.

3

I Created a Morton-stein!

Bad dog! Bad dog!" Joe said firmly.

Sneakers's ears flattened against his head.

"How did he get in here?" Mr. Hardy cried.

Mrs. Hardy pointed to an open window. "There's your answer," she said.

Frank grabbed a handful of paper towels. He began to wipe up the mess. "Did anyone call the station about Sneakers, Dad?" he asked.

Mr. Hardy shook his head. "Not yet," he said.

"Well, Sneakers," Joe said. "Looks like you're staying with us for a while."

"Just a minute," Mrs. Hardy said. "I didn't say Sneakers can stay."

"Please, Mom," Joe begged. "At least over the weekend, until school starts."

Sneakers padded over to Mrs. Hardy. He began licking her hand.

"Well," Mrs. Hardy said. Then she smiled. "I suppose he can stay for a day or two. But out in the yard."

"And if Sneakers's owners don't turn up by tomorrow night, he goes to the Bayport Animal Shelter," Mr. Hardy said.

Frank and Joe nodded.

"We'd better stock up on some dog food," Mrs. Hardy said. She looked at the meatball mess. "This dog has a *huge* appetite!"

"Sort of like Chet Morton, huh, Mom?" Joe asked.

"No!" Frank said with a groan.

*   *   *

20

After a quick lunch of grilled cheese sandwiches, Frank and Joe decided to make posters about Sneakers.

Joe drew a picture of Sneakers. "Lost dog," he said as he wrote the words at the top of the poster. "Answers to the name of Chet."

"Cut it out, Joe," Frank said.

Mr. Hardy drove the boys around town so that they could hang the posters in store windows and on trees around the neighborhood. When they got home, Sneakers bounded across the front lawn to greet them.

"Sneakers looks restless, Dad," Joe said. "Can we take him for a walk in the park?"

"You can, but you're going to need a leash," Mr. Hardy said. "You don't want him to run away again."

"We don't have a leash, Dad," Frank said. "We've never had a dog, remember?"

"We may not have, but I think the people who owned the house before us had a dog. I remember seeing a leash in the garage. Let's go look."

Frank and Joe followed their father to the garage. Sure enough, they found an old green leash and collar in the corner.

"It looks old, but it will do for now," Mr. Hardy said. He slipped the collar around Sneakers's neck. Then he snapped the collar closed.

Frank and Joe walked Sneakers to the park. Sneakers trotted along the sidewalk. Frank held the leash, and Joe carried a new skateboard under his arm.

"I don't see Mike anywhere," Joe said when they reached the park. "Just Tanya Wilkins."

Tanya was jumping rope with her friends. They were swinging two ropes. The game was called Double Dutch.

"There he is," Frank said, pointing to the water fountain.

"Hey, Mike!" Joe called. "Where's your Beast-o-matic?"

Mike looked up and glanced around

22

nervously. "Not so loud. I don't want any-one to see me."

"Will you calm down?" Frank told Mike. "You didn't turn Chet into a dog."

"That's right," Joe said. He put his skate-board on the ground. "Even if Sneakers did gobble up a whole meatball hero."

"He what?" Mike gulped.

Sneakers gave an excited bark and pulled on the leash.

"Sneakers!" Frank shouted.

But it was too late. Sneakers took off like a rocket. The leash trailed behind him as he ran.

"Oh, no," Joe said. He pointed to an open field. "He's heading for that picnic!"

But Sneakers didn't raid the picnic. In-stead he ran to two boys playing Frisbee.

Sneakers leaped in the air on his hind legs. His neck stretched as he snatched the Frisbee between his teeth.

"Awesome catch, Sneakers!" Joe cried. He rested one foot on his skateboard.

Sneakers returned the Frisbee to the boys. Then he ran back to Frank and Joe.

"Good dog!" Joe said. "You're a real Frisbee—" He stopped in the middle of his sentence and gulped. "—champ," he finished.

"You mean like Chet?" Mike said.

Suddenly, Joe felt his skateboard being yanked out from under his foot.

"Hey!" Joe yelled. He turned to see Zack zooming away on his skateboard.

"Let's get him!" Frank said.

They chased Zack, but he was too fast.

"WOOF!" Sneakers kicked up his legs and raced past the boys.

"Sneakers is going for Zack!" Joe cried.

"Go get him, boy!" Frank cheered.

Sneakers charged behind the stolen skateboard.

"Get lost, you stupid mutt!" Zack yelled over his shoulder.

Sneakers growled. He lunged and caught the cuff of Zack's pants in his teeth.

Zack tumbled off the skateboard. "Mad dog! Mad dog!" he screamed.

Frank, Joe, and Mike ran to Sneakers and gently pulled him off.

"Way to go, Chet!" Mike said. He scratched Sneakers's belly.

Zack stared at Mike. "Did you just call that mutt Chet?" he asked.

"He sure did," Joe said. "Mike turned Chet Morton into a dog with his new invention. It's called the Beast-o-matic."

"Come on, Joe!" Mike said.

"And he'll do it to *you* if you try something stupid again," Joe added.

Zack stood up. "So, Mendez invented something that can turn people into dogs."

"Not just dogs," Joe said quickly. "Elephants, horses, cockroaches—"

"I saw that dorko contraption you had this morning," Zack told Mike.

"Why should you care?" Mike asked.

"Because this is just like the story about Frankenstein," Zack said. "But this time, you created a Morton-stein."

"I did not!" Mike cried.

"Mad scientist! Mad scientist!" Zack chanted.

"What if the Beast-o-matic really did work?" Joe asked Zack. "What are you going to do about it?"

"Hmm. Let's see," Zack said. He scratched his head as he thought. "I know! I'll tell the six o'clock news on TV. They'd love a story about a mad scientist right here in Bayport."

"Why would a TV station listen to you?" Joe sneered.

"Because my uncle Ed is a cameraman at WBAY-TV," Zack said. "He's giving me a tour of the station tomorrow afternoon."

"And what if we prove by tomorrow afternoon that this dog isn't Chet?" Frank asked.

"Prove it," Zack said. "See if that dog passes up a chili burger."

Sneakers growled.

"Tomorrow afternoon," Zack said. "No later."

"I'm doomed," Mike said as Zack stomped away.

"No you're not," Frank said. "We're going to find Sneakers's owners."

"Let's go back to Chet's house and look for more clues," Joe suggested.

A squirrel scurried by. Sneakers barked and tugged on the leash again. This time the collar snapped open. Sneakers began to chase the squirrel. Frank was left holding the empty leash in his hand.

"That dog needs another leash," Mike said when Sneakers stopped to bark up a tree.

"You're right," Joe said. He looked around the park. "I have a great idea!"

Frank and Mike followed Joe to Tanya and her friends.

"Hey, Tanya," Joe called. "How about lending us one of your jump-ropes?"

"Why?" Tanya asked. "Do you boys want to jump?"

Joe shook his head quickly. "We need to make a leash for this dog we found."

Tanya looked at Sneakers and smiled.

"Okay. We'll give you a rope," Tanya said. "As long as you jump in for awhile."

"No way!" Joe said.

"We'll go easy on you," a girl with glasses said. "We'll just use one rope."

The girls began to laugh.

"Come on, Joe," Frank pleaded. "Sneakers really needs a leash."

Tanya and her friend began to swing the rope. "Teddy bear, teddy bear! Turn around!" they sang together.

"Oh, please!" Joe groaned as he jumped in. Suddenly he felt the rope snag his sneaker. It wrapped around his leg like a cowboy's lasso. He went tumbling to the ground.

"Whoa!" Joe yelled.

The girls surrounded Joe.

"I guess you can borrow the rope now," Tanya said. Then she began to laugh.

"Thanks," Joe mumbled.

The boys freed Joe's leg from the jump-rope. Then Frank tied the thin rope very loosely around Sneakers's neck.

"See?" Joe asked. "A perfect fit."

The boys walked Sneakers to Chet's house. There was still no trace of the Mortons.

"If only we can prove that Sneakers came from some other place besides the Mortons' house," Joe said. He stared at the ground as he thought. Suddenly he saw something.

"Check it out," Joe said. "There's a track of paw prints in the dirt."

"Are they dog paws?" Mike asked, holding on to Sneakers's leash.

"Could be," Frank said. He looked at the tracks closely. "The paw prints start from the back bushes . . ."

The boys followed the tracks through the dirt.

". . . and they end up right under the house," Frank finished saying.

Joe gasped. "Right where we found Sneakers!"

"So, that means," Frank said, "that Sneakers didn't come from under the house."

"Maybe Sneakers isn't Chet after all," Mike said.

4

Pampered Pooch

Sneakers tugged hard on his leash.

"Arrrghh! I can't hold him!" Mike yelled. He dropped the leash, and Sneakers ran under the house.

"Sneakers!" Joe shouted. "Come out of there. Now!"

Frank and Joe heard Sneakers whine. Then they heard a strange chattering sound.

"What's going on under there?" Frank asked. He tried to peek under the house.

Suddenly a small raccoon dashed out— followed by Sneakers.

31

Sneakers chased the raccoon through the yard. Then he chased it to the front of the house.

"Sneakers, come back!" Frank yelled.

"The raccoon is climbing into a garbage can," Mike said.

Sneakers jumped up against the garbage can. It began to tip.

"Oh, no!" Joe said.

The can toppled over. Trash spilled all over the ground—and Sneakers.

"Ugh! Gross!" Frank said.

The raccoon peeked out from under the garbage. Then it ran away.

"Sneakers!" Joe called. The boys hurried over. "Are you okay?"

Sneakers shook his trash-covered coat. A clump of sauerkraut hung from his neck. A half-eaten candy bar was stuck to his back.

"Let's clean up this mess," Frank said. The boys picked up the trash and dumped it back in the can.

"Those paw prints probably belonged to the raccoon," Mike said.

"So that means we don't know where Sneakers came from," Joe said.

"Before we look for any more clues," Frank said, "we have to give the dog a bath."

Sneakers let out a loud whine.

"But we've never given a dog a bath before," Joe said.

"Do you have a better idea?" Frank asked.

"He can chase a raccoon through a car wash," Mike said quickly.

"I know!" Joe said. "Mom got a bunch of coupons in the mail. One was for a free visit to Bowser Bliss."

"What's Bowser Bliss?" Frank asked.

"It's a pet place in Bayport," Joe said.

The boys hurried to the Hardys' house. Frank and Joe ran inside. Mike stayed outside in the yard with the smelly Sneakers.

The Hardys found the coupon and got

permission from Mrs. Hardy to walk Sneakers to Bay Street.

"Sneakers must smell worse than we thought," Frank said. People were holding their noses as they passed.

"There's Bowser Bliss," Joe said. He pointed down the street.

The boys led Sneakers to the store. A bell rang over the door as they walked in.

Joe whistled. "Fancy place!"

A girl sat on the couch with a fluffy white dog on her lap. "Eeeew!" she said, and held her nose.

"Can I help you?" a lady sitting behind a desk asked.

"I hope so," Joe said.

Just then a man in a white jacket and black pants came through a beaded curtain. His name, Curtis, was sewn on his jacket.

"Lisa, did you see my Chihuahua clippers?" Curtis asked. He looked at Sneakers. "Yikes! This dog looks like he was in a food fight."

"Nope," Mike said. "A trash can."

"I see, I see," Curtis said as he examined Sneakers.

"All Sneakers needs is a good bath," Frank said. "Right?"

"A bath?" Curtis chuckled. "This dog is a special case. And special cases call for my special treatment."

"What kind of treatment?" Joe asked.

"My very own shampoo of tomato juice, soy sauce, and lemon zest," Curtis said. "Followed by a soothing egg-yolk rinse."

Mike wrinkled his nose. "We want to clean him, Mister. Not eat him."

"It's your only hope," Curtis said. "Unless you enjoy walking a skunk."

Sneakers growled.

"Let's just go for it," Frank said. He untied Sneakers's leash.

Sneakers followed Curtis behind the beaded curtain.

"Don't make him smell *too* good," Joe called. "He's still a dog."

36

The boys sat across from the girl with the white dog. She leaned over and smiled.

"My dog, Colette, is a French poodle," she bragged. "She's won six blue ribbons in dog shows."

"Quick. Pretend to read a magazine," Joe whispered to Frank and Mike.

Frank grabbed a copy of *Calling All Canines* and opened it. The three boys buried their heads inside.

"Here's an article about a Frisbee-catching dog named Baxter," Frank said.

"Sneakers catches Frisbees," Joe said.

"It says that Baxter is missing," Frank said. He turned the page.

The boys stared at a picture of a dog catching a Frisbee.

"It's a golden retriever!" Mike said.

"Are you thinking what I'm thinking?" Frank asked slowly.

Joe gasped. "He looks exactly like Sneakers!"

5

All Washed Up

What else does the article say?" Mike asked.

Joe began to read out loud. " 'While the world searches for the canine champ, Baxter's owners in Bayport wait for news about their pet.' "

"Bayport?" Frank cried. "That's it! Sneakers is really Baxter, the Frisbee-catching dog!"

Mike looked relieved. "Then he may not be Chet after all."

"Excuse me?" Frank asked Lisa, the

woman behind the desk. "Can we borrow this magazine?"

"You can keep it if you'd like," Lisa said. "We're done reading it."

"Thanks," Joe said.

Frank rolled up the magazine and stuck it in his back pocket. "Wait until we show this to Zack. He's going to flip—"

Frank was interrupted by a loud clatter. Suddenly, Sneakers ran out from behind the curtain. He was covered with pink soap suds.

"Sneakers!" Frank shouted.

"He's soaked with tomato juice," Joe said.

Curtis dashed out, waving a towel. "Get back here, you beast!" he shouted.

More soapy dogs slipped past Curtis into the waiting room. One terrier had curlers on her head. A bulldog was wearing a plastic shower cap.

Sneakers shook pink soap suds all over the waiting room. "Yuck!" Joe cried. The

walls and furniture were covered with pink splats.

"Let's get Sneakers!" Frank screamed.

"It won't be easy!" Joe shouted.

Bubbles floated in the air as the dogs chased each other around the coffee table.

"Frank," Joe called. "Throw me the gummy worms!"

Frank reached into his pocket and tossed Joe the bag of candy.

"Oh, Sneakers," Joe called, waving a wiggly worm in the air. "Come and get 'em!"

Sneakers turned his head. In a flash, the soapy dog was in front of Joe, jumping for the gummy worm.

"Don't let him eat it!" Frank shouted. "Candy isn't good for dogs!"

Joe popped the gummy worm into his own mouth. Then Frank slipped the jump-rope leash around Sneakers's neck.

"It's all Sneakers's fault!" Curtis cried as he scooped the bulldog under his arm. "I never met a dog who hates to have his hair washed as much as he does."

The boys looked at one another.

"Hey," Mike asked. "Doesn't Chet hate to have his hair washed?"

"Let's get out of here," Frank ordered. He tugged on Sneakers's leash.

"Your dog smells much better now!" the girl called as the boys ran out the door.

"Thanks!" Joe called back.

Frank, Joe, and Mike brought Sneakers back to the Hardys' house. They tried to rinse Sneakers in their front yard.

Frank chased Sneakers with a garden hose.

"I'm going to invent a shampoo for dogs," Mike said as he sat against a tree. "It'll smell like dog food. I'll call it Scrub and Grub."

"You know what, Frank?" Joe asked as he tried to dry Sneakers with a towel. "We're getting more clues that Sneakers is Chet than clues that he's not."

Sneakers barked as the Hardys' friend Tony Prito came into the yard.

"Don't tell Tony about the Beast-o-matic," Mike whispered. "Too many people know already."

"Okay, okay," Joe whispered back.

"Hi, Tony!" Frank called.

Tony was usually very cheerful. But today he looked sad.

"Great dog," Tony said, rubbing Sneakers's neck.

"His name is Sneakers," Joe said. "We found him."

"Where?" Tony asked.

Mike jumped behind Tony and waved his arms in the air.

"Around town," Frank said quickly.

"Hey, Tony," Joe said. "Why don't we introduce Sneakers to your dog, Boof?"

"Don't mention Boof," Tony groaned.

"Why not?" Mike asked.

"Boof has a stomachache from eating a hot pepper from my dad's plate," Tony said. "The vet said he'll be okay by Monday."

"That's good," Frank said.

"Not!" Tony said. "Boof was supposed to be on *Man's Best Friend* tomorrow."

"You mean that neat TV show where dogs play games for prizes?" Frank asked.

"That's the one," Tony said. "Boof was going to run through the obstacle course. Now I have to call the station to tell them we can't make it."

Joe's face lit up. "Why don't you use Sneakers for the show?"

"Does he run fast?" Tony asked.

"Ask Curtis at Bowser Bliss." Frank laughed.

"If Sneakers is on TV tomorrow," Mike said, "maybe his real owners will recognize him and call the station."

"Hmm," Frank said as he thought. "And if he's Baxter, the Frisbee-catching dog, then everybody will recognize him."

"What do you say, Tony?" Joe asked.

"Well, I guess another dog is better than no dog," Tony said.

"Now you're talking," Joe said.

"Bring Sneakers to WBAY tomorrow

morning at nine. I'll be waiting there with my mom and dad," Tony said.

"Hear that, Chet?" Mike said to the dog. "You're going to be on TV."

Tony stared at Mike. "Did you just call him Chet?"

Frank shook his head. "It's a long story, Tony. A long story."

After dinner Frank and Joe went outside to feed Sneakers. It was just getting dark.

"The show tomorrow is just the beginning," Joe said. "After that will come dog food commercials. And movies—"

Sneakers looked up from his dog dish. "Grr," he growled

"What is it, boy?" Joe asked quietly.

Sneakers ran to the hedge surrounding the yard. He began to bark.

"Who is it?" Frank called out into the dark. "Who's there?"

A shadowy figure popped up from the bushes. Frank and Joe screamed.

6

Chaos on the Set

Say 'cheese'!" the figure called.

"Zack!" Joe shouted.

"In person," Zack said. He was holding a camera. He aimed it at Sneakers and snapped. The flash made Sneakers whine.

"What are you doing?" Frank demanded.

"Just taking a souvenir," Zack said, pulling the instant film from the camera. "From my visit with the Morton-stein monster."

Joe reached over the hedge. He tried to

grab the picture. But Zack had jumped on his bike. He was already riding away.

"Remember, Clues Brothers," Zack called as he pedaled, "you have until tomorrow afternoon to prove that the mutt isn't Chet. Or else WBAY-TV is going to get an awesome news story."

When Zack was gone, Joe knelt down next to Sneakers. "I wish you could talk. Then you could tell us who you *really* are."

Just before bedtime the boys decided to call the Mortons' house, to see if Chet was home.

"No answer," Frank said. He put down the receiver.

Joe yawned. "Let's hit the sack. I'm *dog* tired."

"Very funny," Frank said as they trudged upstairs to their rooms.

The next morning Mr. Hardy drove Frank, Joe, Mike, and Sneakers to WBAY.

Tony and his parents were waiting for them outside.

"He looks like a champ," Mr. Prito said as he ruffled Sneakers's fur.

Mrs. Prito sniffed the air. "He smells like tomato juice," she said.

After Tony walked Sneakers backstage, the boys followed Mr. and Mrs. Prito into the studio.

"A real television show. Neat!" Joe said as they found their seats in the audience.

Frank looked around the television studio. There were thick wires on the floor and lights hanging from the ceiling. Three cameras surrounded a colorful set.

"There's the obstacle course!" Joe said excitedly.

"And there are Tony and Sneakers!" Mike said. He pointed to the side of the set.

Frank wasn't paying attention. He was too busy flipping through *Calling All Canines*.

"Are you reading that article again?" Mike asked Frank.

Frank nodded. "I'm almost sure that Sneakers is Baxter, the Frisbee-catching dog."

Suddenly the bright lights flashed on.

"The show is about to begin, boys," Mrs. Prito whispered.

"Five . . . four . . ." a woman wearing a headset counted. "Get ready to applaud!"

"Ladies and gentlemen, boys and girls," an announcer shouted. "Please welcome the host of *Man's Best Friend*, Jack E. Russell!"

Jack Russell trotted out onto the stage. "Hi, folks!" he said. "Welcome to the show where your poodle can win oodles of prizes!"

"Or your golden retriever," Joe whispered.

"But first," Jack went on, "I want to introduce our special canine celebrity guest. He's fast. He's furry. He's—"

The cameras spun around as a golden retriever sprang from behind a curtain.

"—Baxter, the Frisbee-catching dog!"

The boys' mouths dropped open as the dog caught a Frisbee thrown by Jack.

"Frank," Joe said. "If Sneakers is backstage, and Baxter is out front, that means—"

"But the magazine said Baxter was missing," Mike said.

"Uh-oh," Frank said. He was staring at the front of the magazine. "This issue is over a year old. He was probably found months ago!"

Mike slumped in his seat. "That means Sneakers might be Chet after all."

Baxter caught some Frisbees thrown by people in the audience. Then he bowed his head and ran back through the curtain.

"Baxter sure likes to put on the dog, doesn't he, folks?" Jack asked the cheering audience. "Who's our first contestant, Carol?"

A woman dressed in a dalmatian-spotted dress handed Jack a blue card.

"Jack, our first contestant is Tony Prito and his dog, Sneakers," Carol said.

"Woo! Woo! Woo!" Joe hooted as Tony and Sneakers ran onto the set.

"Hi, Tony," Jack said. He looked down at the card. "It says here that Sneakers is a stray dog."

"That's right, Jack," Tony said. "My friends found him right here in Bayport."

Jack turned to the camera. "Folks, if you recognize Sneakers, please call station WBAY."

Then Jack winked. "But not until after the show—so Tony can win a new CD stereo unit with four speakers!"

The audience clapped wildly.

"In order to win," Jack explained, "Sneakers must jump through the rubber tires, roll in the confetti, chew the giant slipper, ring the bell with his teeth, and last but not least, eat the treat that our assistant, Carol, is holding at the end."

"Got it," Tony said.

"Then take your place at the obstacle course and wait for the buzzer," Jack said.

Tony led Sneakers to the obstacle course. Sneakers's ears shot up as the buzzer sounded.

"Look at him go!" Joe shouted.

"He's jumping through the tires!" Frank yelled.

"He's ringing the bell!" Mike cried.

"Sneakers has ten seconds left to eat the doggy treat. Ten seconds!" Jack cried.

"Sneakers! Sneakers! Sneakers!" the audience chanted.

Sneakers sniffed the treat in Carol's hand. Then he jumped back.

"What's he doing?" Frank asked.

Sneakers whined. He dropped to floor and rolled on his back.

"He's not eating it!" Joe cried.

"Scarf it down, you big bowser!" Mr. Prito shouted.

A loud bell rang.

"Aw!" the audience moaned.

"Oh, I'm so sorry, Tony," Jack said. "Sneakers didn't win."

"B-b-but . . ." Tony stammered.

"I guess this is one dog who doesn't like liver," Jack said. He pointed to the doggy treat.

"Doesn't Chet hate liver?" Mike asked.

"More proof!" Joe cried. "That does it. I'll bet Sneakers really is Chet!"

The boys watched as Tony and Sneakers were led off the set.

The Pritos drove the boys home in their minivan.

Tony and Mike sat in the middle seat. Frank and Joe sat in the back with Sneakers between them.

"That dog made a monkey out of me on national TV!" Tony groaned.

Joe bit his lip. He couldn't keep Mike's secret any longer.

"It wasn't Sneakers's fault, Tony," Joe insisted.

"How come?" Tony asked glumly.

"Because Sneakers . . . might not be Sneakers," Joe answered.

"Joe!" Mike cried. "You promised not to tell!"

"Are you boys keeping secrets back there?" Mrs. Prito called from the front seat.

Joe took a deep breath. He put his arm around Sneakers and told Tony everything.

"You mean Mike's Beast-o-matic might have worked?" Tony asked, his eyes wide.

"Why else would Chet be missing since yesterday afternoon?" Joe asked.

"But he's not," Tony said.

"What do you mean?" Frank asked.

Tony shrugged. "I saw Chet and his family yesterday afternoon—at Pizza Paradise."

7

Clues and Chews

You saw the Mortons?" Frank asked Tony.

Tony nodded. "On my way home from the library yesterday."

"Was Chet there, too?" Mike asked.

Tony stared at Mike. "Duh! Would Chet pass up a chance to eat pizza?"

"Do you know the exact time you saw them?" Frank asked.

"Sometime between twelve and one o'clock," Tony said. "Why?"

Frank squeezed his eyes shut and thought hard. "We found Sneakers at exactly twelve-thirty. I remember looking at my watch. If the Mortons were at Pizza Paradise, then—"

"—it means Sneakers can't be Chet!" Mike said happily.

Mr. Prito pulled the minivan up to the Hardys' house. Frank and Joe climbed out of the van. Sneakers hopped to the ground.

"Hey, guys!" Tony called from the window. "Even though Sneakers did lose, thanks for letting me use him."

"Thanks for the clue!" Frank called back.

When they got inside, Frank and Joe tried calling Chet again. There was still no answer.

Sneakers stayed in the yard while the Hardy family ate lunch in the kitchen.

"Did you watch Sneakers on TV?" Frank asked his parents.

"Not only did we watch the show," Mrs. Hardy said, "we taped it."

Mr. Hardy put down his tuna sandwich.

"Speaking of tapes, I have to go to the office today to watch some security videos."

"From where?" Frank asked.

"Mr. Park from the Quick Shop thinks money was stolen from his register," Mr. Hardy said. "I offered to look into it as a favor. I thought I would start by looking at the security tape."

"If there was a thief, will you see him on the video?" Joe asked his dad.

"Not only that," Mr. Hardy said. "The tape will also show the exact time of the crime."

Frank was about to bite into his sandwich when he stopped. "Dad, do you think Pizza Paradise has a security camera?"

"If they're like most stores, they probably do," Mr. Hardy said.

The boys finished their sandwiches. After helping to clear the table, they went into the den.

"Maybe the Mortons are on the security video," Frank said. "Then we'll know what time they were at Pizza Paradise."

Joe tossed his Gross Ghost figure in the air. "And if they were there after twelve-thirty, then Sneakers can't be Chet."

"I'm sure Kevin's mom will let us watch the security video," Frank said.

Kevin Saris's parents owned Pizza Paradise. Kevin was also Frank and Joe's friend.

Frank and Joe got permission to ride their bikes to Pizza Paradise. They called Mike and made plans to meet him there.

Sneakers jumped up on Frank as the boys left the house.

"Down, boy!" Frank called. He fell back on the door and felt something crunch behind his back.

"Someone hung up a picture of the Frankenstein monster," Joe said. He put his Gross Ghost on the doorstep.

Underneath the picture, in Zack's handwriting, were the words "Time is running out!"

"I hate to admit it," Frank said, "but Zack is right. Time *is* running out."

The boys left Sneakers on the doorstep and hurried to their bikes. They rode to Pizza Paradise. Mike was waiting for them outside.

"There's Kevin," Joe said as they entered the pizza place.

Kevin looked up from the garlic knots he was helping his parents twist. "Hi, guys! Want some pizza?"

Mrs. Saris smiled. "We have a pizza pie topped with cherries and pineapples today."

Joe kept himself from making a face. "No thanks, Mrs. Saris."

Frank explained why they needed to see the security video.

"I'm not sure I understand how Chet can turn into a dog," Mrs. Saris said. "But you're welcome to watch the video."

Mrs. Saris led the boys to the back room. She took a tape off a shelf and popped it into the VCR. Then she left.

"There's the time clock in the corner of the screen," Kevin said as he started the tape. "We opened the store at eleven-thirty in the morning."

Kevin fast-forwarded the tape until the first customers came in at 11:40. "It's the Bayport girls' soccer team," he said. "They always order fifteen meatball heros to go."

A few seconds later, Joe asked Kevin to stop the tape. "There's our dad buying our two-foot hero."

Kevin fast-forwarded the tape again.

"Stop!" Frank said. "I see something!"

The boys stared at the screen.

"It's Chet and his family!" Joe cried.

"It looks like Chet and Iola are fighting over something," Mike said.

"Chet wanted pepperoni," Kevin explained. "Iola wanted sausage."

Joe moved closer to the screen. "It says it was . . . twelve P.M."

"That's a whole half hour before we found Sneakers," Frank said. "It doesn't prove anything."

"Chet could have turned into a dog by then," Joe said.

"What do we do now?" Mike wailed. "In just a few hours, Zack will tell the whole town that I'm a mad scientist!"

"Calm down," Frank said. "If we can't prove that Sneakers isn't Chet, then we can still find his real owners."

"I'm going home," Mike said. "I have to work on a new invention."

Frank and Joe rode home. Sneakers wagged his tail when he saw them.

"Hi, pal," Joe said to Sneakers.

"He's chewing on something," Frank said. He tugged at a small piece of blue paper hanging from Sneakers's mouth. Sneakers wagged it back and forth before letting Frank have it.

Joe's heart pounded. "Oh, no! It looks like . . . like . . ."

He ran to the doorstep. There was his Gross Ghost—crunched into tiny pieces!

"Bad dog!" Joe shouted. "Bad dog!"

8

Lost and Found!

That was my favorite action figure," Joe said. He felt a thick lump in his throat.

Sneakers looked up with big, sad eyes.

"Sorry, Joe," Frank said. "Sneakers was just being a dog."

Joe nodded. "And that's *all* he is."

"What do you mean?" Frank asked.

"Chet would never break my Gross Ghost," Joe explained. "Best friends don't do things like that."

Suddenly they heard someone snicker. It was Zack riding his bike past their house.

"Time's up, Hardys!" Zack yelled.

"Where are you going?" Frank shouted.

"To the TV station!" Zack shouted back. "It's time the world knew about the mad scientists of Bayport!"

"Let's follow him," Frank said to Joe. They hopped back on their bikes and chased Zack all the way to WBAY-TV.

"Can I help you?" a guard asked as the boys filed through the big glass doors.

"My uncle Ed is giving me a tour of the station today," Zack said.

The guard smiled. "Ed is expecting you. Go down the hall to the newsroom."

Zack made a mean face at Frank and Joe. Then he ran down the hall.

"We're with him," Joe told the guard.

"Have fun!" The guard smiled.

Frank and Joe chased Zack down the hall and into the newsroom.

The big room was filled with reporters working on computers. Behind the report-ers Frank and Joe could see the the long desk where the newscasters sat. Off to one side was the weather map.

"Hi, Zack," a man called from across the room. "Ready for your tour?"

"In a sec, Uncle Ed," Zack said.

The Hardys watched as Zack jumped up on a chair. He held up the picture of Sneakers. "Attention, everybody!" he shouted.

"Oh, brother," Frank groaned.

"I bring you major news from right here in Bayport!" Zack went on.

Uncle Ed looked embarrassed. "Zack? What's going on?"

"This dog used to be a boy named Chet!" Zack shouted out. "There's a mad scientist in Bayport, and his name is—"

Just then the door swung open. Jack E. Russell walked in with a gray-haired woman.

"It's Jack!" Joe cried.

"Hello, boys," Jack said.

The woman stared at the picture. "It's him," she cried. "It's my dear Rascal!"

"Huh?" Zack said.

"Kids, meet Mrs. Cortez," Jack said. "She watched *Man's Best Friend* this morning. She recognized Sneakers as her lost dog."

Joe's mouth dropped open. "He's your dog?"

"But why didn't he have a collar?" Frank asked Mrs. Cortez.

"I took Rascal's collar off yesterday morning when I tried to give him a bath," Mrs. Cortez said. "That's when he ran away. Rascal hates baths."

Frank and Joe stared at each other.

"Rascal shmascal," Zack snapped. "This dog is really a kid named Chet Morton."

A reporter snickered. "That sounds like a story for the *Bayport Blabber*."

The other reporters laughed, too.

Zack turned bright red. "Ha-ha," he muttered. He got down from the chair and marched out the door.

Frank turned to Mrs. Cortez. "Sneakers— I mean Rascal—is over at our house. We're sure going to miss him."

"Then why don't you keep Rascal for the rest of the day?" Mrs. Cortez said.

"Really?" Joe asked.

"Just give me your phone number. I'll call your parents and arrange to pick him up after dinner," Mrs. Cortez said.

Frank wrote their phone number on a piece of paper and handed it to Mrs. Cortez. Then he turned to Joe.

"That solves the mystery of Sneakers," Frank said. "But it doesn't tell us where Chet and the Mortons are."

"How would you guys like a tour of the newsroom?" Zack's uncle Ed asked.

"You bet!" Joe said.

"I can't believe you're related to Zack," Frank told Uncle Ed. "You're so nice!"

They followed Uncle Ed to the news set. Uncle Ed showed the boys the control room with its twelve TV monitors. They even got to sit behind the news desk.

"Where do you get your news stories?"

Frank asked as he looked through a camera.

"Sometimes they come up on the computers," Ed explained. "And sometimes stories come through the fax machine."

"Look," Joe said. He pointed to a fax machine nearby. "There's one now."

Ed handed Joe the paper. "Why don't you read it?"

Joe began to read: " 'A fourth-grader from Bayport has won the annual hot dog eating contest at Whiz-Bang Amusement Park.' "

"And here's a picture of him," Ed said as he pulled out another paper.

Frank and Joe stared at the picture of the grinning boy holding a huge trophy.

"It's Chet!" Frank gasped.

"It *is* Chet!" Joe cried. "Hot dog!"

After thanking Zack's uncle Ed for the tour, the Hardys hurried home.

"Let's call Mike and tell him that we found Sneakers's owner and Chet," Frank said as they parked their bikes.

"We don't have to," Joe said. "There's Mike now."

Mike was standing in the Hardys' yard. He was pointing another gadget at Rascal. "I'm going to pull this switch," he said. "And you will turn back into Chet."

Rascal barked and ran behind a tree. All of a sudden, the door to the Hardys' house opened.

"Hey, guys," Chet said as he walked out. "Your mom makes great tuna fish."

"Ahh!" Mike screamed.

"What's with you?" Chet asked Mike.

Frank walked over to Chet. "Why didn't you tell us yesterday that you were going to Whiz-Bang Amusement Park?" he demanded.

Chet shrugged. "I didn't know until the last minute. I was upset about my Frisbee, so I guess my folks felt sorry for me."

"So?" Joe asked.

"They surprised me and Iola with a trip to Whiz-Bang for the whole weekend. We stayed in a motel with a pool—and a snack bar right in the room."

"How come you didn't let us know you were going away?" Joe asked.

"I did," Chet insisted. "I stuck a note in your mailbox. Didn't you see it?"

"No," Joe admitted.

"I slipped it inside your Gross Ghost fan club magazine," Chet told Joe. "You always read it right away."

Joe slapped his forehead. "No wonder I didn't see the note. I haven't read the magazine yet."

Frank turned to Joe and Mike. "Well," he said, "I guess this case is officially and finally solved."

"And I'm not a mad scientist," Mike cried happily. "Yeee-haaaa!"

Frank, Joe, and Mike gave one another high-fives.

Chet scratched his head. "Case? Mad scientist?"

Rascal jumped out from behind the tree. He wagged his feathery tail.

"Say, guys," Chet asked. "Did anything weird happen while I was away?"

Frank looked at Joe and laughed. "Nothing out of the ordinary," he said.

"Yeah," Joe said. He knelt down and gave Rascal a pat. "Nothing the Clues Brothers couldn't handle!"

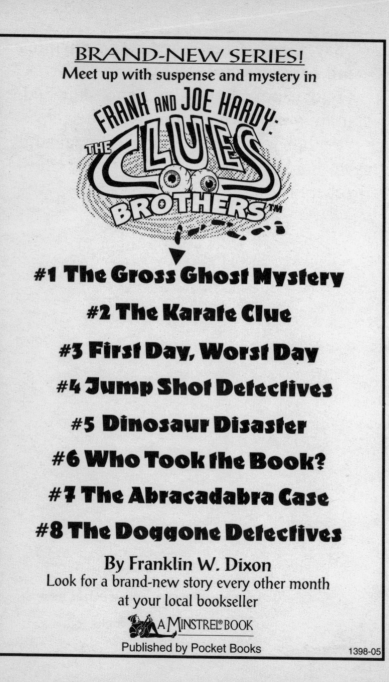

BRAND-NEW SERIES!

Meet up with suspense and mystery in

FRANK AND JOE HARDY: THE CLUES BROTHERS™

By Franklin W. Dixon

Look for a brand-new story every other month
at your local bookseller

A MINSTREL® BOOK

Published by Pocket Books

1398-05

Do your younger brothers and sisters want to read books like yours?

Let them know there are books just for them!

THE NANCY DREW NOTEBOOKS®

Look for a brand-new story every other month

Available from Minstrel® Books
Published by Pocket Books   1356-01

TAKE A RIDE
WITH THE KIDS ON BUS FIVE!

Natalie Adams and James Penny have just started
third grade. They like their teacher, and they like
Maple Street School. The only trouble is, they have
to ride bad old Bus Five to get there!

#1 THE BAD NEWS BULLY
Can Natalie and James stop the bully on Bus Five?

#2 WILD MAN AT THE WHEEL
When Mr. Balter calls in sick,
the kids get some strange new drivers.

#3 FINDERS KEEPERS
The kids on Bus Five keep losing things.
Is there a thief on board?

#4 I SURVIVED ON BUS FIVE
Bad luck turns into big fun
when Bus Five breaks down in a rainstorm.

BY MARCIA LEONARD
ILLUSTRATED BY JULIE DURRELL

 A MINSTREL® BOOK

Published by Pocket Books

1237-04